THE MIRABELLE PICKERS

By Jacques Réda in English translation

POETRY

Treading Lightly
Selected Poems 1961–1975
translated by Jennie Feldman

PROSE

The Ruins of Paris
translated by Mark Treharne

Jacques Réda

The Mirabelle Pickers

Translated by
Jennie Feldman

ANVIL PRESS POETRY

Published in 2012
by Anvil Press Poetry Ltd
Neptune House 70 Royal Hill London SE10 8RF
www.anvilpresspoetry.com

Cover drawing by Jacques Réda

This book is published with financial assistance
from Arts Council England

Designed and set in Monotype Bembo by Anvil
Printed and bound in Great Britain
by Hobbs the Printers Ltd

ISBN 978 0 85646 449 2

A catalogue record for this book
is available from the British Library

Contents

Friday Night

LEAVING the heart of the Upper Saône region and with half the journey behind me, I find myself riding along roads lined with plum orchards, the mirabelles ripening in abundance this time of the year. And busy as the pickers are, they also keep a wary lookout. If you stop, so do they: a hundred pairs of unblinking eyes scrutinize you till you move on. I don't especially look like a fruit-raider, but then nothing about me categorically rules it out. They have the cars under surveillance too. It wouldn't take a minute to fill a basket stowed in the boot, and I am equipped with two tell-tale saddle-bags. On the verges are mirabelles that have simply dropped, the bliss of fulfilment merging with the laws of gravity, their blond perfection enticing. But even though slightly bruised they are destined for the barrel and hence no less untouchable than the others. I wouldn't be allowed so much as a plum stone.

That is how I see my home region: a kind of forbidden fruit. The very fruit that stands as its emblem and whose fragrance, at least, is offered up on gusts of wind.

IT's already late when I reach the crest of Xermaménil. The view extends for six or seven kilometres in a panoramic sweep across the flat town and its environs, on a plain dusted with brightness. At its centre, like two upright elderly ladies in dusky pink finery, are the spires of Saint-Jacques, framed by an arch of majestic trees in the foreground. At this point I have to confess that – however incongruous it might seem, and just as on a summer's evening a cool breeze or sudden dampness can make one shiver – I find myself absurdly shaken by sobs. But with quite a few cars still going by, full of craning necks, I pull myself together and launch, red-eyed, into the descent.

And I try to figure the reason for such emotion: maybe the overlong day on the road, or an intuitive sense that these rare return journeys, which once carried the thrill of an ever-renewable triumph, would from now on be numbered. Lastly, though, it may be in response to seeing my home town again, given my peculiar attachment to it.

THERE it is, the place where I came into the world through an entirely chance combination of circumstances. Logic suggests I should have been born elsewhere (in Burgundy or Piedmont or Paris), but restlessness had driven my ancestors along unpredictable paths. Had it been otherwise, I would certainly have had a different father or mother and – just as I am only a fraction of what I might have been – I would then have been less than half of what I am. In short, I would have been someone else, a notion that invariably unsettles me, though this sort of calculation inclines one to believe that in any case (even more unsettling, I think) one is always someone else.

But this small, chance event that would prove fateful – my birth – did indeed take place here, on one of these streets I am slowly riding through, every detail familiar. All of them are utterly deserted. Not a single figure to be seen between the square by the railway station and the end of Rue des Capucins, not even a youngster skipping home from the only bakery still open. Nothing but houses, the fronts radiant in the setting sun, the backs plunged in the semi-darkness of a theatre with its lights dimmed or about to go up. Nothing but space: this is where, given a generous welcome and decent quarters, space comes into its own, testing itself from street to street, luxuriating in the park and rearing up in the town squares before resuming its course with greater assurance. More civilized, that is. For it can wreak havoc, too. Crossing Rue d'Alsace, which runs due east through iron-flat suburbs, I thought of those districts, so strung out they are torn between paralysis and headlong flight, unable to contain or absorb the relentless concentric thrust that so alarms them. Having done away with its ramparts before the time of Louis XIV, the town did not think to counter this kind of danger by drawing itself in; on the contrary, holding fast to the land and to its fate in the field, it had fanned out and entrenched itself encampment-style on the horizon, with only the two stiff yet graceful towers rising to serve as rallying points; the houses are rarely permitted more than two stories. Behind them are walled-off gardens or vast yards with great sheds, hangars, workshops and vegetable plots. The town itself is hollow, like a lead soldier, and – apart from the older, more compact neighbourhood near the main church, where pastel shades of renovation give the place a theatrical look, especially in the evening – it seems to accommodate within its walls and façades as much space as is held on the outside, the street patterns creating a system of sluices between the two. But you didn't actually live at the centre of this exchange, for there was no mid-point: nothing but edges and outlines, which left you wondering which side of the town you were on and so made the place seem both real and artificial. At every turn you had to take your bearings afresh, the effect being one of perpetual surprise. What I recognize above all is not so much the familiar features of this town, which has barely changed, as the astonishment it inspired in me, and still does.

One Sunday, for reasons I cannot recall, I had been put in the care of our housekeeper. Not knowing what to do with me, she had stuck to her usual routine and then taken me to vespers at her parish church, Saint-Maur, in a neighbourhood I had probably never visited. During the service night had fallen, and there we were, walking through streets that looked unfamiliar yet at the same time rather similar to the ones I took every day, though they too resisted the effects of habit. The town was a baffling yet protective place – singular yet duplicate – where you could not really get lost even though it slipped away from you on all sides. As I ride through it this evening, it offers the same enigma, and although I feel an almost physical delight in the sense of being at home, there is still something I cannot grasp. But meanwhile I have made myself late.

LAST-MINUTE compunction: in Bayon I stopped at a public telephone to call Marie and tell her I was on my way. A six-year absence, promises unkept and all the signs of having forgotten her, and now I would be arriving in about an hour. Fine, she would be waiting for me. Things were always straightforward with Marie. She wouldn't hear of anyone putting up at a hotel and kept a special room for all relatives passing through. One of the first things she did was to give me the key. Now the two of us are having supper in the little kitchen at the far end of the apartment where my parents lived for several months after their wedding, and from which she, once married, never moved. Everything – the furniture, the rustic plates on the walls – is still in place, recovering its substance through the haze of memory. Across the stillness come the shouts of my cousins trooping through, the debonair voice of Georges and the hubbub of family feasts for which he copied out the menus in his meticulous longhand. Back then, too, there was the same stillness, floating on the arpeggios of Mademoiselle Emilienne from two floors up; it was the very substance of the town with its spacious parks, one of which I can see if I lean towards the window. This was the other side of the stage set. From here you can make out in the distance the backs of houses that bear no apparent relation to their fronts on Rue Carnot, being more like the reverse side of a different town I would never know.

We tell each other our news. I keep losing track of names and ages, and Marie could easily catch me out for not knowing – not caring, that is, after so many years spent elsewhere, on different planets, turning up only now and then with the aplomb of the eternally prodigal nephew assured of his rights. But she doesn't bother with such reckonings; smiling, she asks for another drop of wine. Neither of us feels the need to keep saying "Do you remember?" – it would be almost indecent, and anyway unnecessary. The past comes unbidden, quivering and transparent, and in it Marie's face is as smooth and soft as it was then. I think of an old photo where she's striking an ecstatic pose in the role of Saint Thérèse of Lisieux. If I mention it, I know she'll laugh. And as if we had followed the same broken train of thought, she tells me how much the church's theatre club had helped her find her feet when she was young. A moment later the subject is the new baby born to one of Line's daughters, and a postcard that came the day before from Italy or the Island of Oleron. Nowhere is there any trace of planning or perspective, no bitterness or resignation, and no regret; rather, an ever-present intimacy with all that has been, and with all that lingers on inhabiting the moment in image-form, a kind of heavenly bubble where the living mingle with those who have vanished. These memories are not in the least dizzying, and don't call for the kind of downward plunge that has one spluttering for the surface. It's as though she is gathering them from the air, like tame birds, and if their wings cast a shadow when she is alone, it is a strictly private matter and I will never be the wiser. When she does, suddenly, single out something – so tactfully that I am spared any embarrassment – it is the most intimate of all: she reads out an old letter, the first she ever received from Georges, where he declares his love in a tone of solemn restraint. More than a letter, it is a pledge and a plan of action, carried out so faithfully that there would have been little scope for the selfish misgivings that can lurk in sadness. Georges was definitely not a hero. Something better, perhaps: "a good man," says Marie, who prefers to keep things low-key. And she adds: "I was lucky. The two most important men in my life (for me there were only ever those two: my father and my husband), and I couldn't have found better." I, too, am sure of it. I can see Georges now – sometimes troubled, often busy – but with a rotund frankness always verging on a smile. Out of this apparently monotonous existence of his he would extract anecdotes that he developed and flavoured exquisitely (he was also a fine cook), ever attentive to life's achievements, which had no worth unless shared with others. He was the quintessential man of that town, and through him it looked very different from what I saw in the grip of my diehard solitary ways.

What do I find most intriguing of all? Not Marie's words, nor the evident trust they convey, but the fact that she is dry-eyed. There was a time when she couldn't relate the most trifling or comical of anecdotes without the tears welling and streaming down. Now she hasn't even pulled out a handkerchief. She lapses into silence for a while, smiling, lost in hazy recollection; when she turns to me, her eyes are shining. Night has fallen meanwhile.

THIS room – which within minutes of my unpacking has the look of a gypsy encampment – this room opening onto the silent street is where my youngest cousin stayed before he left for America, later returning to Paris to die by misadventure. Or rather, out of compunction. It is hard for me to say more. I was travelling at the time, and maybe, looking back, I went too far in respecting his intense privacy. We lived in the same building, but he remained elusive, as if invisible. Our last meeting had been quite by chance, one evening outside the baker's, between the shadowy crossroads and the golden glow of bread. That was where we really discovered each other again. I left next morning filled with a sense of relief. I have since come to realize how little one should trust one's impressions. Seeing that there have already been quite a few tears shed in these pages, I don't mind including those I wept on my return when I learned what had happened. As someone who readily snivels over his own fate, I rose somewhat in my own esteem after that bout of sobbing. It was like a dam bursting from the weight of a brute grief that would have been unbearable had it not suddenly – through some merciful magic involving the instinct for survival – become a hurtling torrent. The very force of the flood makes it short-lived; a half-hour later, all is dry. But then it takes years to grasp the extent of the devastation. For although

Pascal and I did not know each other very well, there were all kinds of similarities between us, enhanced by a brotherly spirit. He was born almost eight years after I left the town with my parents, and it was as if, through him, I had lived out the rest of my childhood there, and my adolescence. On several occasions during his own youth I had seen him pitting his unusual talents against the stifling provincialism. Whereas my knowledge of the town had been shaped and skewed by juvenile fascination, his experience of it was much broader and would, I rather naively hoped, be passed on to me. Yet in the brief excitement of my return visits, whatever it was that stirred in me feelings of nostalgia and enduring astonishment, produced in him nothing, ultimately, but an anguished sense of being engulfed, and a desperate urge to escape. I remember how one night we stopped outside a shoe shop that hadn't changed in forty years and seemed to have exactly the same slippers on display. This constancy, which I found quite touching, appalled him. Another evening he took me to an abandoned country-house some way out of town and led me into the courtyard. With the aid of loudspeakers, projectors and old hangings he had created a kind of opera stage, with explosions of colour and Wagnerian thunder reverberating against the decrepit façade. It wasn't long before the entire set-up collapsed and we then went to look in the wings – rooms strewn with rubble but still quite majestic – in the process rousing an enormous sow. Anxious to protect the brood that could be seen foraging in a corner, she charged at us, grunting in pursuit as we sought refuge in the car. The whole unplanned interlude took Pascal by surprise no less than me. For he had given up this kind of fantastic spectacle some while back, letting his theatre fall into disuse along with the country-house. Perhaps, though without counting on the supporting role of a family of pigs, he had wanted me to understand how the need to quit the town for a different kind of solitude, for some – any – other, imaginary place, could drive one a bit crazy. There was only one way to deal with it. And so he left.

Looking through what remains of his book collection, which has been ravaged by hordes of curious nieces and nephews, I listen to the mute town enveloping me as once it imprisoned him. What would I have done in his place, I wonder? What was it like for him to come back here? – Here, for him, meant above all Marie, not the town he had decided to leave behind; I, on the other hand, was taken away from it and am drawn back to its maternal presence. But what kind of mother can the town really be? I've pushed open the great wooden shutters to let her in, and turned out the lamp. Soon we will share a single sleep.

Saturday Morning

I WAS up early to organize my things, and since there might be quite a crowd this evening, went shopping for Marie at the supermarkets. The town has two of them, one set up near the school by our friend Auguste. Like everyone else, I like to declare my fondness for small-scale commerce – not to speak of the open market, which happens to be held today in Place Léopold – but much to my own disapproval, I cannot resist the appeal of those anonymous stores. Standing in their aisles, I could be anywhere – Beauvais, Créteil, Cahors. At least that's what the distracted shopper thinks. But one soon becomes aware of subtle differences; the same goes for the produce, despite the trend to standardize. I remember the lovely cloth-bound exercise books I once bought in Nice and have never found anywhere since, search as I might. Wines, as well, and beers, and inedible cheeses that were still worth buying for their naive or grotesque labels. There is something else, too, but it's only by positioning yourself near the tills during slack spells that you learn of it. For that's when the cashier ladies, old and young, take advantage of the brief respite

– when the "boss" herself relaxes her vigilance – to chat among themselves, or with a woman shopper, about life's ups and downs. By pretending to be engrossed in some special offer, you can pick up passages straight from a novel; much of the time, it's true, these are no more distinctive than the interchangeable stock on the shelves – but not always. Sometimes you come upon a remarkable flair for story-telling, which transposes the banality of the tale into something lyrical. And then, largely thanks to the more or less outlandish regional locutions and accents, standing out as they do against the impersonal outfits and surroundings, you find yourself back in a human context. Curious but timid, I was standing rather too far away this morning as I listened to one such cashier conversation. I couldn't make out what they were discussing, but was struck, all the same, by the recurrence of a typical sonority, or rather *sonoritay*, which will all too soon disappear (*disappayre*), and which, as I gazed over their heads at the *shoppayng* in full swing, brought back memories of Madame Lalitte, the farmer's wife.

In keeping with some principle or tradition, we always bought our weekly butter from her and no one else, and since in those days my mother was always busy in the shop, it was delivered to our door – big, one-pound oblong blocks of yellow embellished with mouldings of fruits and flowers. When we cut from it we would leave untouched, for as long as possible, the decoration I found so delightful. But it was Madame Lalitte herself who delighted me even more. She was an apparition from another realm, not only from the heart of the countryside that you could see from Rue Banaudon or from the far bank of the bathing-place, but out of some fabulous world. With her straw hat, rustic skirts and baskets, and her resonant singsong voice (such is the Lorraine accent), she was a decidedly quaint figure, but my joyous amazement whenever she burst in was nothing short of mythic. Her appearance symbolized light, space and fecundity, and although she must have been ugly – the monumental body, the hard-baked face – she had the kind of beauty a goddess conceals beneath a crude exterior lest we be dazzled. With her came the brilliant world of the immortals, sweeping through our kitchen in that uneventful town. But along with these recollections of Madame Lalitte comes another abiding image – at once realistic and divine – that is all the more vivid for existing solely in the mind's eye. One day she described how, walking from the bus-stop to her village with the sun in her eyes, she would often stop at the same spot and stand there to pee on the road – "just like a cow," remarked my mother. Yes, like a cow, but right into the sun's red orb, a noisy torrent upon the vast roof of the world.

AT LUNCH Marie is beaming. The morning has brought an abundance of mail: a letter from her daughter, a postcard from her son-in-law – a rotund hoarder and purveyor of knowledge, humour and energy, known to all as "the rector" – who is busy exploring Carolingian crypts in Swabia or the Palatinate, and two more cards, from Gérard's sons in America. Then Yves phoned from the Vendée, and his brother (Gérard, that is) called to say he would be arriving soon. These messages have in turn absorbed several others, covering almost entirely the vast, shifting family tableau. Marie is surrounded by a whole network of busy affection. Even though we are just the two of us in this kitchen, where once I was the primary focus of her love, I suddenly feel an outsider. To be sure, I have my own family (and Marie is always asking after them), but with her I am like an only son; it is a matter on which everyone has their own view, or else reserves judgment. If we were still animals, there would be times when we quietly huddled against each other. Sadly, all that remains of such an instinct is something that – to the benefit of language – urges us to mistrust it; though having monopolized it so long for my own use, I might have tied the tongues, as it were, of my own children. Without a true centre, we are bound to have the cautious or superficial relationships of distant relatives. And when you are standing on the sidelines, what could be more attractive than those groups where, beneath the turbulence and wrangling, you have the sense of something woven into a binding strength that nothing can tear apart? That is no doubt another reason for my attachment to this town. All the same, I know I would go back there even if everyone had left and reconnected their circle elsewhere. But had Marie ever thought of moving away? "Heavens no," she says. "It's so good here." And then, after a moment's pause, another "No", in a tone full of thoughtful conviction – weighty, resonant – that leaves me feeling profoundly at peace.

Saturday Afternoon

JUST as I am wondering whether to read or have a rest, my cousin Gérard appears and resolves the matter. We exchange kisses, he being my godson; in any case, it comes naturally. Not so with his older brother, whom I will not be seeing this year and who detests this particular social convention. To keep me at a distance he always seizes my hand firmly and leans well back for safety's sake. Sometimes I tease him by insisting all the same, which upsets him since affection is not the issue. Gérard is altogether uncomplicated. Without further ado he suggests we go plum-picking. They have kept old Scherer's large orchard outside the town, on the south-facing slope at Méhon. I have been there on other occasions with Yves (the one who refuses to kiss) but only for walks. Now there's work to be done. We leave right away, stopping to pick up Gérard's father-in-law. Monsieur Vuillaume has a flourishing garden where I admire the various fruits and vegetables, although the plot (he makes a point of saying) isn't "too well" maintained. That's an exaggeration. And besides, I find the profusion entrancing.

Once up in the orchard, we spread large sheets of transparent plastic under the trees. Not all the plums here are fully ripe. You have to shake the branches vigorously using a long pole at the end of which Gérard has attached a metal hook. And down comes a hail of the ripest fruit, rolling in all directions. Tossing away the bad ones, we gather them into baskets that are soon full. Vuillaume keeps up a nonstop commentary, always to the point and sometimes quite trenchant. Gérard, as is his wont, remains taciturn. For my part, I prove myself a diligent worker, rather gratified to be in the role of those who had eyed me all along the road yesterday. Sad to say, hardly anyone goes by. Before we head back down the hill (it has been just two hours but I'm almost ready to drop), Vuillaume says: Let's go for a walk, stretch our legs. And suddenly, just where the road curves, there are the Vosges mountains under a silent sky.

THOUGH I took the work seriously, I did not by any means stint myself, sinking my teeth into the most irresistible plums. And not only mirabelles: the orchard also had quetsches and greengages. It was the greengage plums I feasted on most, even though few were fully ripe. They are so unlike mirabelles, you could easily think them a different fruit altogether (though these days the name is used commercially to refer only to a kind of plum fed to pigs). The very look of them is delectable: great yellow pearls, their smoothness slightly freckled, and beneath that lustre, a pulp as dense as puréed sun. Plump and firm, some have already burst open as if overfilled with contentment, and the moment you taste them they dissolve, as Valéry puts it, into sensuous delight, much like ripe womanhood in love, the luminous fullness of flesh intimately linked to secret juices of the most exquisite kind.

WITH Monsieur Vuillaume in mind, I keep to myself my observation on the "silent" sky. Although I barely know him, I suspect – from the thoughts he has been voicing almost without pause throughout our picking – that he is inclined to be critical and contrary. Here's the proof: I say out loud, in a cautious tone, "It's a Sunday sort of sky"; back comes his retort: "Today is Saturday." No matter. I really do mean silent. Not that some skies are noisy, but there is a certain kind of light that explodes and expands with nothing to stop it, seeming to rebound and reverberate from even the slightest surface – a stem of wild oats, a pebble. But with night still far off and no sign of its approach, the light this evening stays held in the sky by long, unmoving banks of painted-on cloud. The silence comes from the painting, but also from the painted town below us; down from the sky and up from the town, at one and the same time. The air holds no echo. If the bells were to chime the hour from the ornamental steeples of Saint-Jacques, the five or six strokes would hang in the air, a floating resonance on this pooled silence that stretches to the horizon.

SUDDENLY I feel a twinge of anxiety. All day I have been grateful for the absence of wasps – most unusual for the season – but I have eaten some of the windfall plums lying in the grass, where a few grazing sheep are competently doing the job of a lawnmower. Their droppings, though, are everywhere, and these can contaminate the fruit with the dangerous fluke-worm parasite. The thought grips me briefly, but then seems so out of place and bothersome – already I can see the look Vuillaume will shoot at me if I say something – that it simply dissolves into the serenity of the scene. We set off for the town below. Another stop at the garden that is "not too well" tended, at the far end of which stands the cemetery wall. Vuillaume makes a point of praising his neighbours' placidity. His wife, who has been pottering among the flower-beds during our absence, listens to him with mingled irony and affection. Good-looking, serious and intelligent, she is entirely at the service of this rather eccentric man, who is both inconsistent and

28

reasonable, and whose restless dumbshow, sometimes verging on the sorrowful, is at odds with the constant stream of verbal whimsy. I think he wants to be liked. That's why he is provocative, though always within the bounds of good sense. And perhaps he suffers from being undervalued. Often when he gives his views – on the town in particular (as if somehow wanting to score points over me), but also on many other subjects that come up in the conversation – he reveals in piecemeal fashion a knowledge that is almost encyclopaedic. He worked for fifty years in a library of sorts: did he read everything?

I ACCOMPANY Gérard to the garage. With the return of the warm season, he often comes from the suburbs of his home town, Metz, to spend weekends here. The garage is a small building that our grandfather put up, slightly askew, on a dead-end lane – L'Impasse – on part of a plot that the two brothers later divided between them. Their respective areas are demarcated by lines that remain somewhat theoretical. On one side stands Yves's house, white and spacious; on the other, the old garage, augmented by recent additions I will describe in a moment. When you go in . . . But first let's not forget the mirabelles in the back of the Renault. I ate more of them on the way here. The flavour is peculiarly theirs, an early hint of the alcohol that will be extracted from them; the fruit on the branch has already distilled that subtle, volatile vigour. Two or three heaped basketfuls are tipped into the barrel that stands outside the garage; of the remaining plums, those still left on Sunday will go into jars. That done, we step into the garage. The inside looks like a junk shop: a single glance takes in hundreds of jumbled objects of various shapes and sizes, dating from different periods and destined for every kind of purpose. Some go back to when the place was built, or at least to my childhood. I recognize the Hutchinson poster, with the gentleman in the battered hat, spotted shirt and braces, sharpening a knife on an air-pressure tool that shoots out sparks. But there are also oil drums, planks of wood, sacks, bits of furniture, horseshoes,

enormous nails, bunches of keys, old clothes, helmets, more posters (Técalémit, Castrol, La Française-Diamant),

incomprehensible tools, ladders, books, bricks, onions, newspapers, shoes,

engravings, vases, bicycle wheels, the wheel of a truck, and probably a lighthouse lamp as well and a few stuffed deer.

The stock-taking could go on, but you give up. Gérard himself scarcely bothers with it, though he seems to know perfectly the history and provenance of every scrap in his expanding collection. There is a kind of scepticism in the way he keeps searching for something he might already have come upon but then lost again in the chaos. From the orchard he has brought back a piece of root that looks just like a rat. Before finding a place for it on, say, an anvil or the handle of a whip, he thrusts it daintily under his wife's nose. Florence's unruffled response leaves us disappointed. She is busy peeling vegetables and invites me to have supper with them here, since Marie is feeling tired and has cancelled plans for the evening. I leave Gérard rummaging in the tiny kitchen, and go out to look at the new additions. What they offer would make for a fairly comfortable existence. I survey the beds, tables, shower, stove, toilets. There isn't much space, it's true, but you can always be out-of-doors in the summer. Between these small cabins and the wall of the barracks – still topped with the convulsive barbed wire I remember – there are a good twelve or thirteen square metres of open ground, with a willow tree, grass, and an awning against rain and sun. I couldn't have dreamed up a better retreat: behind a disused garage, on a dead-end road, in a town that is itself rather detached from the bustle of its times. I go into the pocket-size kitchen plot that abuts the boundary-line, hoping to see the tortoise I am told lives there. About the same size as the adjoining ornamental garden, it has hardly anything growing in it. The tortoise has gone to the neighbour's for sustenance. I consider the contrast between them: here, it is almost no-man's land; there, a version of Hollywood. It must be rather pleasant to have Yves's way of life, but I would rather live as Gérard does. After dinner, where I learn a lot about the water that comes by way of sandstone from the Vosges and from prehistory (Florence is a geologist), Gérard searches in a drawer and produces a bicycle bell of the sort once offered to clients of Établissements Réda.

Sunday

A BICYCLE bell is a good start, but some day I would like to look at a whole bike and know for sure it's a Réda, the make as plainly visible on the frame as it is on the covers of books that will sooner or later meet the same fate. With this idea in mind, I set out on a radiant morning in the direction of the castle, to visit the small bicycle museum nearby (almost opposite the library where Monsieur Vuillaume used to work). It was created by a former bicycle manufacturer and he is still in charge of the place. Although older than me, the cap-wearing curator had known only my father, who by that time had stopped manufacturing, defeated by competition from the big firms. "Ah no," he tells me, "we don't have a single Réda." Then, perhaps out of politeness, he adds, "But I have seen some. They are still around, the question is where? In a cellar, in a barn . . . If ever you're coming back this way . . ." But now I can't possibly leave the place without going inside.

The museum is by no means small. Piled into long, narrow attic-like rooms on two floors are hundreds of bicycles and motor cycles of every kind, all of them – so it says on the leaflet I've been given – in working order, even though a few of the models date back to the end of the nineteenth century, and many are from the start of the twentieth. Here is the Lallemend bicycle (1865), minus pedals, the Terrot tandem with double steering and an eight-speed gearbox (1908), the daring Onoto for a threesome – a gentleman and two ladies (1935). Outnumbering these are the motorized machines, an incredible variety of them. You can see how much thought, from the outset, went into locating the optimal centre of gravity, taking account of aerodynamics and the ever-tricky problem of the fuel tank. The most powerful models, designed to perfect the double intoxication of noise and speed, stand side by side with vehicles – some of them three-wheelers – conceived for the rider who puts comfort first. I note the Motobécane (1924) for ladies and clerics, which chugs along quite elegantly, though its cylinder charge (175 cm³) would require the wearing of, respectively, a divided skirt or a biretta with chin-strap. Needless to say, I take a particular interest in the evolution of my own type of bike, which will soon become – even in its most advanced form – a museum piece as obsolete as the Lallemend, as phantasmal as the Réda.

The good smell of oil has me thinking back to the workshop. If I hadn't left this town, what would I have produced? Is there some kind of logic in the process by which a dunce in mechanics like myself has come to project through space the very same posture as that of a sedentary, inventive forebear? Yet after twenty years on the road without a single breakdown or puncture – thanks to what tutelage? – I am beginning to note the first signs of malfunction; the mechanism is playing up and the creature it carries is less responsive. To think I am reviewing the story of my life in this museum, that having travelled in every direction, not wanting to know where I was going, I have finally ended up at my destination – which I had seen as just another stop along the way – thus closing the circle that has brought me back to my starting-point.

Exacerbated by all this sparkling, dead metal, the heat intensifies. Floorboards creak with my every solitary step. Perhaps somewhere out there in the countryside there's a kid on an old bike discovered in the corner of a barn, its label faded, and he's racing ahead full tilt.

THE shortest route takes me, inevitably, past Les Bosquets. Quickly, then, keeping my eyes on the ground. But I haven't written to anyone for several days now, so perching on a bench I take out the postcards bought at the bicycle museum and write a series of banal formulae: love from, warmest regards ... The thought of the real letter waiting to be written, of everything I shall have to put into it, numbs the mind and the hand. And I hastily fill the little rectangle with words of affection, as if taking a deep breath of oxygen before the dive.

THEY are still having lunch back at the garage – behind it, that is, under the awning. The large table can seat seven quite comfortably: Marie, Florence, Gérard, the Vuillaumes, Monsieur Jean and myself. I don't know who Monsieur Jean is, no doubt some relative of distant relations of the Vuillaumes. At ninety, though he looks fifteen years younger, he is a confirmed bachelor. His outfit and his manner are perfectly – even excessively – correct. Everyone shows him the greatest respect. As he is not very talkative (though he seems to listen, for the most part approvingly), Monsieur Vuillaume speaks up on his behalf in full oratorical style. In this way I learn that Monsieur Jean lives in town, his house set in a beautiful garden where he would never dream of setting foot, not for anything in the world. Vuillaume recounts this as though it were the most delightful whim. Monsieur Jean makes no comment. He gazes right through us, eyes fixed on what he can make out (or not) in his garden. He is probably one of those who has never left the town, and he must have known a great deal about the power it exerts before it seized him and settled in his bones. Now he knows nothing. Behind the panes, he has shifted into stupefaction. Hence the unease he arouses in me. I wonder if I wasn't once as wise and old as he is, and if I haven't kept something of that; I am wary, too, of the well-being I feel catching up with me at the same time. It's also the heat and the drawn-out dinner. Vuillaume is the only one still holding forth, somewhat heroically. He has never left the place either, but I have the sense that, with his paradoxes, the flower-beds he tends "not too well" and his outbursts that, however crude, will often be for the benefit of someone else (references to him on several later occasions will give me some idea of his merits), he has never given up the struggle, whereas the other has buried himself in the scenery of his garden. And as for myself – never in one place or another – what am I doing here, with my own portable window?

Finally cake and coffee are brought to the table, and mirabelles. Monsieur Jean must be getting bored with his window; maybe he will take his leave. But no, everyone lapses instead into his dazed state. Not a breath, not a sound. The silence merges with the wide-open spaces congealing around this open-air nook. If a bell were to ring out, would I be alarmed? I remember being frightened by the Sunday bells, huddled down in a corner with my lead soldiers. A fear tinged with sweetness, as now. At long last the ladies stir. They beg us not to go. But Gérard has the sense to rouse himself. "Come on," he says to me, "I'm taking you to the Vosges." Let's go.

IT IS an artificial lake, quite recently excavated by dyna-miting. The grey rock is raw, the water blacker than the fir trees choking the slopes all around. Monsieur Vuillaume, who insisted on coming with us and knows everything, explains to me that this huge reservoir is filled by pumping from the rivers on the plain, so as to release cold water into the Moselle when the tem-perature rises downstream from the power station at Cattenom. A curious system, but it makes me think: we operate in much the same way. When the works begin to overheat, we send along cold water piped from the source and stored in the well of memory. Does this happen with all our mental processes? Maybe some such deep-seated impulse explains the large number of visitors here, for the site itself is rather sinister. Gérard suggests somewhat half-heartedly that we go on a little into the mountain itself, now that we know all about it. But we choose instead to return to the town before night falls.

WITH their plum-stoning operation in full swing, the three ladies exclaim on our return: Back already? It's a while since Florence took Monsieur Jean back to his window, and here we are in the little garden, all six of us around the table. It's that hour of the day when the light suddenly – almost imperceptibly – shatters and retreats across a soft immensity. In the afternoon, time had felt suspended, resting its full weight on us; moving on now, it seems to touch nothing as it goes, forgetting. Soon the illusion will fade. No matter. For a brief while we have paused here as if forever, saying little, picking absently at the leftovers from lunch, passing around a bottle that never empties. And I tell myself earthly paradise has not been lost, that it can, surely, be preserved in the heart of this hushed town where every day we took more or less the same dreamy routes and made the same gestures, and our voices would lift like the clatter of wood-pigeons' wings. But now it's becoming hard to make out the faces. Marie has slipped away, so discreetly that I didn't notice. Next, Madame Vuillaume disappears and my cousins start getting ready to go. I am the last to leave, with Vuillaume. It is dark. When we reach what used to be the pork butcher's shop owned by my other grandfather, we part ways rather abruptly. He goes off with a purposeful stride, but his head gives little restless jerks. What is he thinking about? Maybe he too is wondering what I might be thinking, planted there in the middle of the crossroads.

Monday Morning

OUT early, I head straight for Les Bosquets and enter the park through a side gate. We would come almost every day even in winter, arriving in a cloud at first, under the great fuzzy, fluffy kaleidoscope that swirled around the landau or the pram, across the watery canvas of things reduced to their colours. Here and there, vague shapes that one soaked up like blotting-paper gradually became more defined, startling as they emerged out of the mist. Later, with bucket and spade, we took possession of the centre of the world which – beyond the bench and the pond with its two swans, one black, one white – soon lost its substance: a world in pieces dissolving in a milky solution the moment you moved away only to stumble on others who were suddenly, no less intensely, there; a thousand pieces discovered one by one but in the end fitting together to lay out a single space. And then it was the time of bicycles, mounted forays into the unknown at the far end of the Cyclists' Path, heading towards another boundary, and beyond it to yet another stretch of chaos like the one you had only just subdued. Then one evening you had finally come to a halt, stunned in

the dazzle of light: the world of the park had been con-
quered, but all of it now seemed like those points that
would not yield and drew us back obsessively.

Next to the gate stands a small square structure,
maybe a toll-house or an old fountain. But it looks the
way I had always seen it, neglected, its bull's-eye
window staring shattered onto a hoard of silence and
shadow. I'll never know quite what was inside, other
than an emptiness that still entices and repels me, as does
the basement of the bandstand in the middle of the
park, with its narrow iron door and its casements reveal-
ing a broken-off witches' sabbath with tortured chairs
amid the planks and plaster rubble. On the roofed plat-
form above, I rediscover the palpable, tingling vibration
to be had by shouting or stamping. And I stamp and
shout. Further off, something that even then was a mere
trace amid grimy, overhanging branches has me search-
ing in vain – for the wide ring of sparser, shorter grass
that marked the magic circle into which no one ven-
tured without bravado or a thrill of fear. But its disap-
pearance has not resolved the enigma. There is another
that comes to mind: the bowers, torn down to give a
better view of the castle. That mystery, however, was
much less esoteric. Even with all the uncertainties and
mistakes, you were on the right track: whatever it was
that made paired-off women and soldiers linger for so
long in the greenery of those chambers, had to be
(though in some other, inconceivable way that was surely

a bit repulsive) the same fierce shudder ending in torpor, the same taste of slightly acidified time that you would prolong in secret behind the curtains, under a table, in a corridor alcove – and which you'd have liked to savour there as well perhaps, had you dared to enter the leafy half-light with its quivering birds; if you hadn't so often changed your mind, all of a sudden, because the world is vast and you want to keep running.

For there was another space – quite unlike that of the park, which was bound by railings – the true and inexhaustible space that opened up opposite the castle between two German cannons, trophies from the Great War: the military parade ground, where the squadrons would send clouds of grey and yellow billowing into the air. Nothing, it seemed – just a light wash of roofs and trees showing the village of Chanteheux – could stop the momentum of this military plain bounding eastward to the steppes. The air above it had the electric charge of a frontier, with invisible banners flying in the wind. Sheer space, future, glory... Just as two minutes earlier there had been a furtive thrill in skulking around the bowers, now you were flushed with the headiness of battle. Bearing down on an army with your drawn sword, you cut it to pieces, and pierced through the heart you fell with a cry of "Vive la France!", only to recover the moment you touched the sacred dust.

The parade ground has all but disappeared and the cavalry gone, and this morning no one else is around as

I stroll through the park between the statues of Emile
Erckmann and Charles Guérin – the latter positively
funerary, evoking as it does, no matter what the season,
the sense of decline that moved this melancholic poet to
song. I know hardly anything about him (he died
young) and have read little of his work (yesterday a few
pages of selected poems found in the late books of
Pascal), but I don't think I have ever out-sighed or out-
rhymed him on the themes of twilight, autumn, sorrows
or clouds. What small provincial town does not have its
own poet, who says nothing to anyone now, being no
more than a block of silence in a stone frock-coat under
laurel bushes chock-full of cats? Standing before this
monument, its soot-streaked marble pallid as plaster, I
find I am gazing at my own cenotaph, my own gateway
to oblivion. It's best to face the fact: you can think you
have brushed against angels or touched the vortex of
being, and look how you finish up – with a chestnut leaf
poised on your skull, and flanked by two vestals who
crown the lyrics of lust with longing and death. As I
breathe the air where his verses took flight,
I salute a brother and fellow countryman. Poor *solitary
heart*, so genuinely solemn and mournful. *Happy*, he
wrote,

> *Happy the man who lives in simplicity*
> *Never once leaving the walls of the city*
> *Where his folk are waiting, with kin from the past,*
> *For his dust to be one with their ashes, at last.*

44

Those are my feelings too, this morning. How come I didn't end up as this man? And what do others make of him – the likes of Georges, or Monsieur Jean, or Vuillaume, who have all, in their own way, been versions of him?

I go back across the park for a final visit: to the craggy little rock-garden that smelled of mildew and was known as "the cascade" on account of its trickle of water; in the green half-light behind it we would go on massacring each other with daring, dishonourable blows that left us breathless. The girls squealed. We would scurry out of the damp shadows, laughing awkwardly.

LOOKING out from the castle entrance across the steeply sloping quadrangle and the bronze busby of General Lasalle, who died at Wagram at about the same age as Charles Guérin, you find a pleasantly ordinary bucolic landscape: meadows, clumps of trees along the Vezouze, and in the distance woods and fields alternating on gentle slopes. There is no intermediate area between the countryside and the town, which tapered off to a row of small houses marking out a kind of promenade. The sight inspires a keen contentment, the sort you feel when looking at old schoolroom posters that show, side by side, a road and a path, a lake and a volcano, a forest and a desert, or a headland, a gulf

and a swamp. For despite (or because of) being juxta-
posed, they satisfy the viewer's – increasingly nostalgic –
need for a world in which everything has a place, shape
and meaning peculiar to itself, and so acknowledges in
all other things a specific mode of being. The setting for
these encounters lends harmonious order to one's
thinking. It's the kind of landscape King Stanislas might
have surveyed from his high window, as the easy-going
ruler of this province weighed up his response to
Rousseau. The castle had been saved from the dilapida-
tion that followed its partial conversion into barracks
(latterly for motorized dragoons who had swapped
their horses for side-cars and light-tracked vehicles).
Once the lodging place of Voltaire and Montesquieu, it
now accommodates assembly-rooms, a military museum
and various municipal departments.

I must confess I often dream of seeing it restored to
its true purpose, namely, housing the throne and court
of a despot – even more enlightened, of course, than
Stanislas and his predecessors François III and Léopold,
by which I mean that he would have electricity, an es-
sentially republican phenomenon. Such contradictions
don't worry me any more than the attendant fanciful
dreams of independence for the whole district. I have
already replanned this area several times, organizing a
small military parade and public transport (plenty of
trams). And since only a thriving economy could ensure
the viability of such a state, I would base it on the revival

of the prodigiously successful pottery industry and glass-works, for so long the hallmark of the town (along with its dung-boosted strawberries and its lace-making), but also upon the world's enduring infatuation with the local mirabelle plums. And that's as far as my plan goes and my role in it, given the insuperable complications involved but also because I haven't the slightest wish to take the place of this decent despot, nor to hold any position, however modest, in his regime.

I am dreaming, I know; or rather, it's a game. As when I was eight, or fifteen, or forty, I am indulging in the childish vice of make-believe realms. And however much I rub against its façades or earnestly tramp its streets, the town remains an archetype, abetting my utopias. It's no doubt a way of protecting the place from changes that through their impact would affect me too, a way of fixing the idea of it; but there is also the fact that everywhere – as in the juxtaposition of streets and countryside – the town's reality tends towards an essence, towards the pure visual sign that is the stuff of theatre: these real houses are like a stage set fronting this real landscape and its series of rustic panels. The same with the castle, an empty interior through which you can see windows showing yet more windows, or the same ones lit up by an imaginary background of sky caught in mirrors. So how could one help waiting for something to happen? You were always waiting, but with confidence wearing thin. For it seemed as if the event had already taken place – a baffling contradiction: you were the actor, and yet you hadn't witnessed it. You would never quite grasp the meaning of the play.

AMID all these digressions, I have crossed the bridge over the Vezouze and walked around the austere Place des Carmes. If you continue straight, it's the cemetery. Once it was much visited. On fine weekdays I would accompany my grandmother. Aside from the prayers she murmured on arriving and leaving, it was something of a gardening session. We weeded and lugged around watering-cans and pots of flowers. A cheerful sky shone back from the smooth marble tombs, some of them scattered with small, white stones that looked like knuckle bones, sharp-edged and many-sided. And then on Sundays with the full complement: in winter, the men bundled in thick overcoats – the very word is heavy – their shoes crunching the gravel and their voices, once inside the portal, resonating dully as during mass. The black-hatted women, with bouquets, vases and soft cloths for the stone, launch into a whole series of gymnastic exertions, inhibited somewhat by respectfulness and the under-trappings of their Sunday best, but with the same efficient gestures as when dusting a table or straightening a disorderly bed. Practical remarks on the neighbouring graves are exchanged in neutral tones.

Another party goes by and the greetings are restrained, oblique; then everyone falls silent. We stiffen into a row of onions for an eternity, while a dog's continuous barking in the far distance gives the measure of the empty space as if it were a gigantic box. Finally someone sighs or coughs, or jogs the communal immobility by solemnly pulling up a dandelion leaf, and suddenly every hand is busy making the sign of the cross, each in its own time – here and there seeming to beat the measure of some overwhelming music, or else to catch something dirty on the sly, rolling it into a ball and making it disappear, stuffed in a pocket. We move off once more, straggling along, and the same thing starts all over again a little higher up. From there the town appears as it does on one of those postcards my mother keeps stacked in a drawer – the same dust-grey tone, hazy but definitive, halting the drift of clouds and passers-by.

Hours later, wanting to stretch our numb legs we might come back through the outskirts of the town, and walking along the empty streets with their poor, low-roofed houses, the same impression persists, even more acutely perhaps, because now we must be part of the postcard and there's no getting out.

BEFORE I could give it a name, and as yet too young to have anything but a vague notion of what I would later call "time", I sometimes had the feeling it had already come full circle. And if, despite that, one still moved forward – from one day to another that was often much the same, and often thanks to some baffling, exciting prospect ahead (on Sunday we would go fishing, or "soon it'll be Saint Nicholas Day") – it was, more than in terms of duration, across a space that was almost as frozen as in pictures, and even more alluring than the space of the park and the parade ground. Postcards, images on commercial labels and in illustrated newspapers, the stamps in my father's collection – all were openings that enticed without disappointing. Besides, since the town looked just like them, you could, up to a point, step inside such pictures, although the getting in was not easy except in rare moments of sudden, uncontrollable giddiness. Then you would find yourself on the corner of a real street in the picture, and just as you were about to cross, the tiny coloured crystals that composed it would begin to swell and spin, invading the entire space and dispersing the shapes. You were thrust back to the other side. You couldn't leave it any more than the biplane on the stamp from Spanish Morocco could ever meet its counterpart in the sepia sky of the page that held them side by side. Time would not alter their position. And we who, conversely, never stayed in the same place – probably because the picture containing us was bigger, in all its dimensions – landed back each time in the same final moment of a duration that had run its course and yet did not disappear. Like a river beyond its estuary, the duration widened and mingled with an infinite expanse that dissolved and preserved us at one and the same time. And so the only conceivable activity was the game that winds up the very moment it also, endlessly, starts anew. Better still if playing it, which satisfies the need to shake off the torpor of appearances, consists of quietly challenging their secret as well. Not inside pictures, where it can't be reached, but in free-standing objects you can handle and submit to every fascinated whim. In other words, I used to spend hours away from the park – where you went for the dizzy effect of space and movement – busy examining, hefting and variously deploying lead soldiers in manoeuvres that sometimes ended in brutal skirmishes. Because in the end, the compliant inertia of those small shiny objects yields nothing more than the pictures you cannot enter, and even when you use force, they can do nothing but aver their emptiness. When this happens, the surface of the world is once again as flat as a lake, and above the scene of carnage, duration regains its deep, futureless calm.

But being somewhat disconnected, this duration needed – since it supplied the duration of the game – if not a real source, then at least storage basins with inexhaustible reserves, where it could float and be replenished.

THE town had eight military barracks, if you include the castle, some of them close to the centre and spacious enough to accommodate cavalry units. They added to the impression of immensity, not only because they covered such a wide area, but more especially – quite apart from what they concealed behind walls that permitted only rare glimpses – on account of their oddly irregular shape. Instead of occupying a well-defined square or rectangle, they overlapped with the town's layout in a way that made them seem even bigger, as if they were interconnected by hidden short-cuts, opening up an interior space you somehow envisaged as being wider than the already vast expanse you moved in – encompassing it even. This was the impression given by a wall that ran for some twenty metres between my grandmother's garden and one of the barracks. It was quite usual to find footprints in the flowerbeds, left in the night by dragoons who had taken advantage of the unsettling way in which the two expanses could be confused or switched round. But almost as intriguing as the soldiers' clandestine activities was their actual, punctilious presence. Every day when we came out of school in the late afternoon, there they were, strolling along the streets in small groups, often in dejected silence; ghostly emissaries from the realm of the barracks, they could hardly be told apart under their kepis, in the horizon-blue that still served as the uniform. For certain important occasions the town was decked out in blue and jonquil-yellow, the colours of the riflemen who would march past at a rather brisker though more mechanical pace amid splendid brassy reverberations. They would take up position in the square and stand there unmoving except for the brief, jerky movements performed in unison, punctuated by a ragged clicking of bayonets and the single dull thud of rifle-butts. Then they would again turn to stone, and in the compact silence generated by their inert mass you could hear the troopers streaming closer, the brittle air shining with the thrill of trumpets. A momentary quiver, and the mass would ripple into a single column, ready to move on – and then, in a sudden about-turn, head straight into an avalanche of drummers, whereupon there began, despite this counter-weight, the rigid dance of the rifles in which everybody moved "as one man". Plainly, though, they numbered some five hundred or more, and moved not as one man but rather like the same man five hundred times over, and were it not for the concealing shadow of their helmets, you would doubtless have seen, multiplied by a thousand, the same staring eyes painted on the same mould of face.

Given what they knew – as did I, though quite unawares – the soldiers had, like me, only one recourse: play-acting. So as not to dissolve into the infinity of the barrack yards, where they are at the mercy of a duration more unreal and more dead than in town where they will lounge away the evening, they give themselves over to exercises that seem pointless, like much of adult behaviour, but are regulated by a rigorous theatrical precision that corresponds to the version in town and brings events there – in a fit of gaiety – to their apotheosis. Soldiers playing at soldiers, and there it is: the world's why and wherefore made intelligible and justified, as it were, by the game. Or to put it another way, by being amenable to orders that make them go, come back, wheel round or stand where positioned, they have become lead soldiers in a game played by someone or something. And when I play, I am trying to appropriate the power that turns people into lead soldiers. But that other power always beats me to it. The ones my father buys me (and I've known him as a soldier, too, the sort that others obey) are already lead soldiers: they have no liberty for me to overrule in order to make them such, and that's why I sometimes reach the point of smashing them: to see if there isn't, hidden inside the often hollow body, a spark from the life that's eluding me.

In town they were to be found everywhere. Not just in the three or four specialist stores, but in hardware and stationery shops, in groceries, bakeries, haberdasheries and tobacconists. Displays featured a replica of the garrison in all the standard postures and combat positions, as illustrated in the books on warfare that often engrossed me. And there I would again find a postcard monochrome stretching peacefully over ruined villages, forests of limbless trees, dead bodies that would never be buried in the false depths of the page, for like their leaden counterparts, real soldiers were also exposed to outbursts of rage and – unless they were eternally wounded (like the heavily bandaged figure in my ambulance) – to being broken and killed. As with those walks back from the cemetery, it was all taking – or had taken – place in some remote location where you were nonetheless included, with no more freedom of manoeuvre than that of the game itself, so tightly confined, so quickly jeopardized by ennui. In order to spread out and let the game take up all the space, I would have had to add lead soldiers indefinitely, making the leap from that one squadron numbering a few dozen, in better or worse shape, to the full complement; of this, only a fraction was on view in shop windows, and the most coveted specimens always disappeared too soon. Not that they would have done much to help my moody confusion, but the ravages it inflicted could have been made good, forever, had I owned the lot. "Line them up," I was advised, "and just *pretend* to bomb them. Watch how little Robert does it" – the son of a captain, with a collection that remained intact (he later became a colonel), Robert would be shocked by my outbursts of combative frenzy. How, then, to take possession of everything? Not just the lead figures, but the soldiers they represented and that inaccessible space where they always manoeuvred, which in turn encompassed the town that contained my small self? How? There was a way, a method I resorted to on more than one occasion.

It meant leaving my boxes behind. No need even for the soldier outfits given to me for Saint Nicolas Day, and soon destined to meet the same fate as the fragile metal figures. A rifle made of wood, a scrap of cloth transformed into martial headgear, and I am ready. Rigged out thus, I take up my position at the top of the outside stairs leading to the bedrooms, and there I stand on guard, and wait. Ten minutes, an hour. Were I a few years older, people – the grocer crossing the courtyard to his stock-room, the woman lethargically ironing in the house opposite – would think I was crazy. But who can be bothered with the weird ways of kids? They are used to such things, never suspecting that they and the courtyard are being blotted out by that same kid's gaze, just as he cancels himself out – absurdly, madly serious, standing rigid between the outward emptiness and the hollow he embodies. Until ennui fills him to the brim, followed by misery (and he'll have no more idea than anyone else why he was in tears), while at the same time he will have turned into all the lead soldiers, and felt for himself the power that makes them be.

THE delights of boyhood, I think to myself. Could it be – I am now near the entrance to Les Bosquets (right in front of the fine house where the famous treaty of 1801 was signed, humiliating Austria) – that I am making things up? Or perhaps interpreting, complicating, dramatizing? Lost in such musings, I have walked right past the impressive baroque – or rather, rococo – church with its Vosges sandstone colour, which also brings to mind the pinkish cloth of my father's best suit, with my mother calling out (to my father who never knew what to wear, or couldn't care less): "Put on your rosewood!" The poetic ambiguity of *bois de rose* must have intrigued the child (Father floating in a wood of roses). But I registered the expression in terms of its pure phonetic substance: *bwadroz*, like a magic formula turning my industrious father into some kind of larky adventurer.

As for the church, I suppose I should at least have stopped and gone inside, rather than simply glance in and note that, behind a heap of beams and canvas sheets, instead of the greenish plaster of the old days – where the upper reaches were blasted by fanfares of bugles and drums – white and gold were back in favour, silent and triumphant. It is the church of my patron saint, where I was baptized and had my first communion, a supposedly private event, prior to which Father Sarrut, who always had little bubbles of grey foam at the corners of his mouth, distributed an inventory of all the sins normally conceivable at so tender an age. Disobedience, lying, greed, laziness – they had all, true enough, been committed, and it is hardly a coincidence that I have forgotten the exact formulation for the most chronic, and in some ways the most serious, of them all. For although the church did not seem to make any more of it than, say, a case of pilfering or bad temper, the transgression in question did expose one to the full force of the secular authority, being considered a vice that exceeded all the others put together, and more detrimental to family honour than to the serenity of Jesus. But there is also another that comes to mind. It was not mentioned in the standard list, nor considered a capital, culpable offence. Whoever indulged in it was apparently the victim of some deficiency rather than an agent of evil as such, even though he himself was aware, more acutely than at any other time, of an anxiety related to conscious wrongdoing. If Father Sarrut had been more perceptive, if he had read Baudelaire, he would have recognized ennui, brother of pride and intemperance, amid the dirty linen I tipped from my little bag. Perhaps it was beyond his competence in theology and, especially, beyond his benignity. Of course, one can hardly treat the soul of a seven-year-old as a spiritual reality subject to the rigours of casuistry. But what is ennui? It is, decidedly, the sense of being involuntarily set apart. Yet who can know to what extent the person excluded

does not want it that way; if he might not in fact be
clinging, out of desperation, to some earlier verdict of
exclusion? Such questions should not be ruled out
on the supposed grounds of good sense or tender-
heartedness. In short, I suffered a lot from ennui, espe-
cially during High Mass on Sundays, when Lucifer
himself, the Excluded One, was in the background
endlessly walking up and down in the guise of a tall,
thin, moustached beadle in a flowing simar that was half
red and half black, and a truly diabolical cap with red
and black horns – the colours of anarchy, now I come
to think of it, and proof enough that he was the devil,
ironically helping to keep order during divine worship.
I was scared of him, but it felt different from the terror
that struck when the organ let loose the End of the
World and Judgement Day. It wasn't out of any silly fear
that he would kidnap me, nor was I afraid of being pun-
ished for some misdemeanour, since I always watched
my step. But when I saw him, I had a sense of being at
fault because some intuition told me that, despite his
lofty manner, he himself had been punished. However
solemnly he glided over the cold flagstones, he had the
bearing of someone who cannot, should not and does
not wish to find repose. Out of the corner of my eye I
noted that during the elevation of the Host when
everyone else bowed, he continued his little game on
the side, unfazed, his black, brilliant gaze playing
on each of us in turn – the look, at once remote and

shrewd, of a being that cannot be duped and whose indifference is pitiless. What he feels is ennui, he knows that I feel it too, and whatever lies in store for me is of no more, or less, interest to him than if I were about to tumble from a window in the Antipodes.

For my own part, I am of course more interested in the money-box angel in front of the Christmas crib in the same church, which nods a thank-you when you put in five sous, a coin with a hole in. As I do so, my round face is scrutinized to catch – beneath the lank hair and behind the glasses (in my squint) – the effect of a marvellous, simple mechanism that can plunge me, aged four, into a delight which in turn delights the grown-ups. Over the years it comes to be expected, and I guilelessly do the same thing again at twice that age, solely out of self-protection and maybe to make them happy, my face all smiles. It is with the same good will that I stumble through the responses to the catechism, though confronted with the gentle mysteries of the faith, I am basically as doltish and recalcitrant as I will be in later years when faced with the wall of the sol-fa or algebraic equations. In all this prodigious mental drama, it is only the threatening elements that have any effect on me: the beadle with his darkness and blood, the fiery hand in a picture-book Bible that writes on the wall at Balthazar's feast "numbered, weighed, divided". My understanding of religion confirms what the town has taught me: everything has already happened, and no hand will ever erase what a town hall clerk recorded in the registry along with my name: I am on the outside.

But outside meant the town, and it, poor thing, did its best, asking nothing in return and offering somewhere to live.

BY NOW it is late morning. Retracing my steps, I go down Rue des Capucins. It used to have a well-known bakery that somewhat tempered the horror of going to the barber and the tedium of piano lessons. With the first, it was not so much the scissors that I dreaded, as the electric clippers; the second were one long swoon that engulfed the teacher too, a sad and timid lady whose husband collected butterflies. When I came to, there they were, the great trays with their music of colours. On a different day of the week I had drawing lessons where I acquitted myself rather better, notably with a memorable "Capture of the Retinue of Abd-el-Khader". My parents made sacrifices; they had ambitions for me. I could have become an artist like my mother, who in her youth painted roses on velvet. And what am I left with? A fierce longing for a crayon of a particular blue – deep periwinkle, almost violet – and the exquisite pleasure of mixing green and blue to paint a sea I had never laid eyes on. Other than that, I was – I knew it all too well – a failure. It would have taken

more concentration than I could muster, and a perse-
verance that I found humiliating.

Down on the left, still looking Lamartinesque,
though the park it once fronted has been reduced to
nothing, stands the house that I did not know was the
poet's (the man in stone at Les Bosquets). Place Léopold
ahead of me is an open invitation to stroll across, but I
turn right into Rue Banaudon, a short street where
business keeps up a lively pace. I am tempted to say it is
"closed off" by a hill in the distance, but no: here again
you find – it seems to take you by the hand – that
moving encounter between the encompassing town and
the beckoning countryside. This is what was missing in
the nearby capital of the region, a place you went to
only on exceptional occasions. I would come back dazed
by the crowds and bowled over by the trams and the
luxury of the Cooperative Stores, but with a lingering
impression of excess and confusion. Rue Banaudon was
all I needed. Among its more upscale premises was
Maison Scherer – hardware supplies, wallpaper, linoleum,
glass, paints. My uncle Georges was more or less the
manager, *primus inter pares* of a whole tribe of brothers-
and sisters-in-law and their spouses, all of whom some-
how made a living from the business. It was a bustling,
complicated family and I felt a little lost in its midst,
unable to grasp who was related to whom by marrying
into ours – all of which, however, made it fascinating for
an only child like myself. Old Scherer was the patriarch,

an enlightened despot in the manner of Stanislas, and from what I heard he ruled skilfully over this tribe with its turbulent rivalries and jealousies. I had the impression, though, that there was a secret, powerful force holding it together, and something indefinably exotic too. Old Scherer didn't lift a finger. You would often come across him sitting in state outside his door, in the garb that ministers wore at the time – a hat with a turned-up rim, black morning-coat, grey waistcoat, a pale tie, striped trousers – his stomach wedged against his thighs, keeping an eye on everything despite a cloudy vision skewed by cataracts. When he had had enough there, he would take himself off to the café frequented by the local worthies; in its low windows, above the forbidding curtains, you would sometimes catch sight of the bald, doddering head of a dyspeptic waiter. Come evening, the feeble current in the frosted-glass lamps would burnish the copperware and highlight the fold-marks in the white linen. The café, long since gone, had a magnetic attraction of an entirely different order from that of the barracks or certain places in Les Bosquets. It aroused curiosity but kept it at bay; existed powerfully, but as a contradiction. For it was the fact of being ageless that made it seem so brand new, so very present, as if time from a distant past had crystallized in space. You wouldn't dream of actually going inside. The only ones who could take such a liberty were characters like old Scherer who had never known anything but old age; ensconced there forever, they could freely enjoy the privilege, drawing their mysterious energy from the regenerating shadows of that café. And if during their muted conversations it transpired that one of their number had died, there was no proving that the black-plumed funeral carriage and its black-draped horses (with baleful, white-rimmed holes for the eyes) had indeed taken him away to the cemetery. He could just as well have found refuge, once and for all, in the folds of the starched curtains.

Old Scherer's advanced age did not entirely account for the prestige and power he wielded, but it allowed him to do so with minimum effort. He ruled in the manner of one of those robed pashas whose Turkish archetype I had met in pre-War copies of *Illustration*. I think he may have visited Algeria, perhaps even lived there for a while. Everyone went in fear of misinterpreting some gesture or look or half-utterance of his. Being of a different tribe, I barely existed as far as he was concerned, and whenever a family event reinstalled me in his fiefdom for a few hours, I felt – although always respectful, as I had been instructed – not exactly independent but exempt from the constraints imposed on the members of his world. So I was free to observe that world's peculiar customs and habitat.

Part of the store was a back-shop that ran along its entire length, hidden from customers by a rampart of linoleum rolls. A high window let in a neutral brightness here and there unsettled by additional artificial lights that duplicated or diverted the shadows; the overall effect was one of unreality. At the centre of this room, the household – in its widest sense: brothers, sisters-in-law, sons-in-law, nephews and cousins, but also foremen, employees, apprentices, shop assistants – would meet around a very large table for the midday meal. It was accompanied by a continuous coming and going that, far from being chaotic, simply corresponded to the different duties incumbent on each, thereby reinforcing the impression of a respectful gravitation around the patriarch, who was seated at the top end beneath the regal symbol of his hat. I would watch as they craned forward one by one to receive the kiss of trust and good will. My status, luckily, meant only a light pat on the cheek. Most fascinating of all was the gallery that encircled this dining-room like the ground-floor box of a theatre in the round, and served as kitchen, office, living-room and storage area, all at once. Since no one was much concerned with what I did, I could take advantage of the continuous bustle to slip out of my chair and go running along the gallery, where I would position myself behind one of the little columns or in a hidden corner, and from there watch the strange scene around the table. It felt like being in a forest, or more precisely, in the clearing of a forest scene on stage, with those huge rolls of linoleum and their half-vegetal, half-geometric designs, the faint luminosity flecked with other gleams of light and, at the centre, that gathering of men and women – now sitting quietly, now gesticulating – dressed in white or grey and seeming to act out a play whose meaning, although the faces and voices were quite familiar, eluded me. It was a conspiracy in the making, or an episode from Ali Baba. But the scene always ended the same way, with everything falling quiet again and the old boss, his cigar gone out, soon drowsing alone as the savour of stew gradually gave way to the usual blend of linseed oil, soap, varnish and turpentine, a smell so pungent the mere thought brings it back to me, and I can never step into a hardware shop without half-expecting the sudden reappearance of the fantastical clearing where the Scherer tribe held its rite.

BARELY noon, and in any case it's on my way: to get back to Marie's I can take the road past the school. It has only narrowly escaped destruction. Long abandoned and left to decay, it was eventually converted into a residential building, though without any untoward changes on the outside. It occupies about half a block, with two sides on perpendicular streets and the third on Place Léopold. That's where we, the juniors, had our entrance. On one side of that doorway I learned to read, write and count; on the other I picked up the rudiments of history, geography and grammar. There were also lessons of "general instruction", which I remember only too well. One day Monsieur Chancel, a well-meaning if rather tactless man, had chosen me to serve as a live illustration for his lesson on the human body. So: this is the head (forehead, eyes, mouth, etc); these are the shoulders, arms, hands, and so on; and here is the torso: chest, stomach, abdomen – and suddenly, who knows what came over him, in a single swipe he lifts my jumper and shirt and reveals to the entire class, including the girls (sitting on the left), the fact that I wear a corset. And not even one of those orthopaedic undergarments that would rank me with the malformed who can expect pity, but more like something from a window display of ladies' lingerie that one stared and snickered at, with a complicated system of straps and buttonholes to secure the short Bateau trousers we all wore. For Monsieur Chancel, needless to say, there was nothing whatever of note between the navel and the knees. But I turned red as red could be, as if I'd just told a lie. How, then, did one learn about the rest – that mystery, I mean, concealed and yet flaunted in silky window displays? In eighth grade, two years later, there was a brief moment when I thought I had made progress in the matter, thanks to Gristal, the boy who sat next to me in class; he was also the son of a bicycle merchant, and the competition between our parents rather weighed upon any spontaneity between us. But the news was too fresh – and too searing – for him to keep to himself. At the ten o'clock break, he had mistakenly – so he said – gone into the girls' toilets, and he had *seen*. But on his writing-slate, just what he had seen was turning into something chaotic and – it seemed to me – highly improbable, even absurd. It made no sense. Determined to convince me, he kept up the same, lisping insistence: "It'th thtuck on!" What on earth could be stuck on, and if it was indeed "thtuck", what was so amazingly different? He was emphatic but I had stopped listening; I let him go on furiously scribbling the same dubious sketch till his slate was full. I have never seen Gristal since that time and don't know what became of his discovery, nor how he reacted when he came to notice that – unless the case were truly exceptional – it was, in fact, *not* "thtuck on".

Even if he had been right, though, I wouldn't have taken it in. At the time I conceived the thing – maybe I still do – in metaphysical terms. Hypocritical, if you like. For I now believe that Gristal's mistake was not accidental, and give him due credit for having had the courage of his convictions. But like many a naive and impressionable pioneer, he simply could not believe what he had seen. I, on the other hand, did not really want to know. The mystery of girls was rarified into the abstract candour of their knickers, that little patch of soul you caught sight of during skipping or in a gust of wind. Not that I was faint-hearted; I was in love. And despite this highly unsettling localization, I could not have conceived of indulging with her (with Her) in the shameless recidivist impieties that Father Sarrut absentmindedly forgave. – Annette, brunette with blue eyes and a small heart-shaped face, engulfed in abundant fleshiness at the age of sixteen. Let's leave it at that. But a word on Vérine and his gang, who sowed terror at playtime. They would push you back against a tree, while two acolytes grabbed your arms from behind and pulled, to the point of dislocating them. They called this bit of fun by its name: torture, and painful it certainly was. Which brings me back to Annette, because I managed to set up a rival gang so as to dazzle her by defending the persecuted. My reward? A single kiss, by consent, proffered in front of a mirror on an afternoon of childish games, in which she had dressed up as a Chinese lady and I as an Algerian infantryman. This instinctive re-creation of the courtly world most likely ended in hours of detention and a couple of slaps. Not love, a notion that only drew teasing comments – which stung even more, to tell the truth – from the parents, along with something, though heaven knows what, rather suspicious and a bit dirty, that reflected on them too.

I walk round to the back of the school. Opening onto Rue des Bosquets is a gate with the bars and electronic mechanism of a model prison, and through it I can see the entire playground, virtually unchanged, where we loved and suffered; the little terrace with the balustrade that served as the perfect background for school photos. I never look at them. Do I even know where they are? But there's no need. I prefer our airy phantoms, as in the magic beam of the cinema on Saturday afternoons, when the shuddering projector kept up a steady, rasping chuckle amid our gales of laughter. School banished the town, the solitude, the tedium of keeping company with dumb objects. It was where you learned, communally, about the play of passions and their consequences, about the astonishing existence of others. Vérine the torturer, Stuhler (illegitimate and ginger-haired) the victim, Ginette the tell-tale, whether through folly or carelessness, Halftermeyer (who presented me with a pistol given him by his older brother, who had made it from cardboard), Francis who was more than a brother to me, because he wasn't; headmaster Chodorge, a plump, ruddy man with the glaze his name suggests; Madame Ferry, who trained me in literature and gave me a taste for words; Annette, myself, here, right next to the dreadfully hallowed corner where a Polish shoemaker had used his awl fatally to stab Master Schwartzel the bailiff, and the blood had left a great indelible stain on the pavement. We didn't know what to think. We felt sorry for the wretched tradesman facing a seizure that was perhaps unjust, but also for the poor victim who was, after all, an agent of the law. Our views reflected those of our families. For our part, what we felt walking past the blackening stain was nothing more than one of those brief dizzy spells that had us thumping or jostling each other by way of reassurance; if you were on your own, you took to your heels.

Monday Afternoon

MARIE is resting. I may go out in a while and meet her at Zinna's in the evening. Right now it's one of those moments when everything leaves you stranded: an overly raw sky, amnesiac objects, the silence of a provincial early afternoon putting its slow glaze over thought and sight and space. And all of a sudden I recognize the notes that come drifting through the walls like snowflakes from forgotten depths of time. After so many years, I couldn't swear it's the same piano, but it is the same pianist, I'm sure. She has changed her name since, but the old copper plaque affixed at the entrance still says *Mlle Emilienne R.* Now it will stay there as long as the teacher herself. If Emilienne had thought of having a new one put up, during those few months she was to steal from fate, she probably said to herself: "No hurry, let's wait and see." Now it doesn't matter any more. Married at sixty, she has been widowed for more than twenty years. Her story reprises a thousand others, like those monotonous scales coming through the walls.

They had loved each other a long time, but she had an ailing mother and he a sister who was mentally in much the same condition. Resigned rather than patient, they waited. Fifteen, twenty, thirty, forty years. Then the old lady died and the mad sister was sent to an institution. Finally, in a discreet ceremony, Emilienne and Henri were married. Their lives seemed hardly to change. She continued with her piano lessons while he went about his modest duties at the town hall as before. When he came home, though, Emilienne would bustle about in the kitchen putting final loving touches to the meal to surprise him. Having led a fairly Spartan existence, Henri was grateful for this sudden abundance and the marvellous delicacies. So much so that he began to look rather too well, a fact on which he was complimented by everyone, and steeped in this euphoria he dropped dead in the space of a year.

TURNING the corner of Rue Alsace, which is still deserted, I catch sight of her – a small, scurrying ball with curly hair and a tiny hat. I remember what Marie told me: Jeanne is still out and about, always on the run, and if you meet her there's no holding her back: in a rush, can't stop. It must be some natural instinct, as with mice, plus the habit of old times when she used to dash to her milliner's workshop on Rue Banaudon to put the trimmings on a riding-bonnet for a colonel's wife. And although I enjoy Jeanne's chubby little-girl smile – she is unlikely to grow any taller – it's an excellent reason to avoid crossing her path. For far too long she went about telling an old story – passed on by my mother, as it happens – which still amuses her perhaps, if she ever thinks of it now, and which left me uneasy. I was very young at the time, it's true. But I would have preferred the gutter to that bowl, under the gentle but over-attentive gaze of the ladies there, distracted for a moment from their beads and esparto. Today, though, I can't help wondering about them: shut away all day in that workshop amid the rustling of pale ribbons, the wide-blooming artificial flowers and big lacquered cherries? There are at least two explanations, neither of them satisfactory.

Naturally enough, I ended up resenting Jeanne. And if asked why she is forever in a hurry, with no particular reason now, I would say she is paying the penalty for an old indiscretion, her rushing prompted by a constant need to pee.

ALTHOUGH I had not told them I was coming, Antoine and his wife recognize me almost immediately. But they can't get over it, can't quite take in this unexpected, unbelievable apparition that brings with it a whole lost portion of their past. Their faces light up with wonder, their eyes widen. Clearly it is something beyond my present self that they delight in seeing. But I am happy to dissolve into the nimbus they spin around me, as luminous and soft as the wool in the little shop they had next to ours, where the different hues enchanted me. And as I take my leave, I have the sense of waking out of something they have dreamt.

I CROSS Place Léopold and there on the other side – no mistaking him – is Auguste, once our next-door shoe-maker and then, little by little, a major figure in the grocery business. He is rich now, but in the old days I would sometimes help him to roll big barrels of peanut oil, and – to put it laboriously, just as it felt – heave stacks of boxes of tins of sardines from Portugal. Marie told me that one of Auguste's grandsons was finishing his fourth year in medicine: a fine example of diligent metamorphosis from the paring-knife to the lancet. He, on the other hand, has not changed much. Still the superior craftsman at heart, to this day he's as dry as old leather, his salt-and-pepper hair lying neat as fur. But at eighty-eight one is allowed to be short-sighted, and our unexpected encounter in the street leaves him non-plussed. I tell him who I am. He looks me up and down, thinks a moment, and a gleam comes into his eye: "Ah, Jacques," he says, "I didn't recognize you at first. You're looking older."

I WALK with Auguste as far as the Café du Midi where he has his daily bridge party, no doubt in the company of other immortals. As for those who by now have turned into ghosts, just how they disappeared is something I have long known. On Sundays, the day he played cards, my father would sometimes bring me to this very bar, with its ecclesiastically-gilded glass door that seemed to be a solid form of the pungent tobacco and beer smell you breathed inside. I was kept happy with a grenadine syrup or a small glass of beer, courtesy of Eugène, who besides being our regular manservant was a real friend.

It was a rather magical place. Even in gloomy weather the door diffused sunshine, and I found the smoke deliciously fuddling. All I recall now is a player's hands expertly conjuring, dazzling me as he slips a king of spades or queen of hearts across the marble-topped table, where I could make out cloudy skies turned into stone. But what fascinated me even more (and I would crick my neck straining to see) was one of those big nickel-plated spheres standing near the doorway on a stem taller than me. Common in cafés at that time, it was where waiters stowed their cloths and sponges. A pivot mechanism allowed the moving part to slide up and down, and it was constantly opening and closing like a jaw. I can still hear the clank of the metal; I can still see Eugène's automatic but incautious gesture as he stood in front of that dark mouth, which in the end – as it had all the others – swallowed him up.

"DO TRY to go and see her," Marie had said to me. "It would make her so happy." Dry-nurse to the whole of the Scherer tribe, Ninie with her practical jokes and funny faces had made two or three generations of kids roar with laughter, and I had had my share. She has lost the ample bounciness she once had and her mind has dulled. But her gimlet eyes still sparkle. Having exchanged pleasantries we fall silent, intimidated by the impersonal room we're in and disheartened by what lies ahead, unsmiling. But then odd moments of hilarity take hold and shake the whole mass of her: *pouf*, like a sneeze, she remembers. And each time she adds in her cracked voice, "Dear old Jacques, get along with you!" And I say, "Dear old Ninie . . ."

HE IS just coming out of the bar and walking past the fine polychrome statue of Saint Jacques when I recognize Marcel by his wide romanesque-capital smile. Knowing that he had *got an infarction* the previous year, I ask after his health. Not bad, he assures me, not bad.

I just have to go out for walks and so, as you see, I walk. The worst thing is the diet, with three women always keeping an eye on me – my wife and my two daughters, that is, the older one especially, believe me. She's a doctor, and she often just turns up for lunch or supper. So when I've finished my walk, you know what? I stop for a small aperitif with a croissant or a brioche, and then when we sit down to eat, I'm not hungry, of course. I hardly touch the bread or the wine or the sauce. And they're happy. "You see," they say, "you do know how to be sensible, Papa."

I AM just about to turn automatically into the street I have been avoiding since I arrived, when I run into old Wagner. Well before the 1914 war he was my grand-father's book-keeper. Does he remember? Ah, and how! But soon he is telling me instead about some vague episode from his childhood in Alsace; things have become muddled, it seems. Not least because he too has just emerged from a bar – a far better place to be on such a hot day than in the dusty shop he still runs, selling less-than-new furniture. Clearly Sylvaner polish helps to conserve. At ninety-nine, Wagner is as straight as a post topped with a small red apple. By now I'm hardly listening; instead I am gazing at him, lost in thought. Whatever else, he has also drunk the obstacle

of time. With him here, this street where I was born
trails off into uncertainty; nothing ever really happened.
When he takes his leave I have the impression he is
striding across rooftops, the past, the future, worlds that
roll on. He will never die.

I HAVE asked after her, but nobody – not Antoine,
Auguste, Marcel or Wagner – has been able to give me
any information. How can anyone have left so little
trace in such a small town? And why have I put her
beyond memory's reach? I can't retrieve anything of
her voice or her face. Just a vague shape enveloped in
steam. She would iron all day in that long white room
in the company of young women whose stares and
giggles rather unsettled me, amid black stoves cluttered
with irons of different sizes, enormous baskets (called
charpagnes) and swathes of linen that fluttered as if this
was where they mended angels' wings. The wooden
stairway at Madame Karl's made me think of a wind-
mill; I enjoyed playing on the steps. Sometimes I would
be called through the half-open door, or else I went in
by myself. I was hugged and kissed – a little too much,
perhaps – and then seated on a low chair with a box full
of pictures from Tobler chocolates: "Wonders of the
World" – Fujiyama, the Pyramids, Louis Pasteur, the
snow leopard. Madame Karl's white cat would brush

past my knees, all softness, barely discernible in that warm, misty world that even smelt of whiteness.

And yet Madame Karl has not completely vanished. I see her now from behind, carrying one of those baskets covered with a towel. She goes to the far end of the courtyard and stops a few paces from the laundry wall. Then she reaches purposefully into the basket, lifts her arm back and hurls with all her might. Again: reaches in, lifts and hurls. I can't help it: that's the only image that comes, along with the squeals from the little bundles of fur that she's dashing to bits.

I'VE managed to avoid the street, but not the memories, and hurrying to my next meeting, I find myself thinking of Fernand.

Pink, powdered and affable, scented with an eau-de-cologne as rare and forthright as a newly-bound book, he always dressed with an elegance that flaunted his good taste (refined studies in beige and, especially, pearl-grey, with everything matching perfectly, from the gloves and gaiters to the hat). He would cross the street to greet my ever-laughing mother or my father with his grease-blackened hands, bestowing kisses with relish. Then he would set off at a brisk pace, light cane in hand; perhaps, I used to think to myself, the same sword-cane he had carried in Paris, back in the days when a rash word was still, on occasion, reason enough for a duel. And could even land you in prison, if in your political zeal you clashed with the cops. But on reaching his prime, Fernand had abandoned the tumult of the boulevard and newspaper offices for his true capital, and here, married and father of a family, he enjoyed quiet repute between Place Léopold, Les Bosquets, and the café the notables frequented. His stories and opinions were savoured in the local press. An indulgent philosophizer (especially where his own philosophy was concerned), he had a gentle, ironic sensitivity to the oddities, the good sense and the antics of "our folk". That was the title of a volume in which he collected various sketches, tales and comic episodes. Growing up between the woodpile and the dung-heap, those emblems of the Lorraine countryside, he could speak the near-extinct local dialect, and his words were strongly tinged with the singsong rural accent.

He used to work in a library, and because I was his son's best friend, I was sometimes allowed to venture inside, as if into a sanctuary. Not that Fernand was the pontificating sort. On the contrary, he was a modest man, all kindness and good humour. The place itself, with its gilt-edged rows of books, filled me with a sense of secret, majestic splendour. I must have made a more or less explicit comparison between the muffled semi-darkness of that retreat and the cruder dimness that prevailed in my father's workshop. And despite the charm

of the big, cluttered work-benches, the smell of solder-
ing, of dirty oil and rubber and iron filings, despite the
fire in the small forge where I sometimes worked the
bellows – my mind was made up early on: I would be a
writer like Fernand.

But what would I write, with no library and no
desk? I had already prepared the cover and folded the
pages for my first book, and I even had the title and sub-
ject: *The Fear* – a fear that had seized me when Marie,
for a joke, had me believe we were lost after one of our
walks. But the pages remained desperately white. It is
to Fernand, though, that I owe the first vague notion
of what I might some day, perhaps, capture in words.
Namely, moments like the one that's still vivid, a good
half-century on: in the distance he is chatting with our
mothers on a June evening at the little refreshment bar
known as the Tivoli, deep inside the park. Under the
great trees, amid a trilling of blackbirds that sundered
the air like silk stretched across a deeper world, you
could make out their laughter and murmurs, the ex-
pressive arcs of the raconteur's gestures tracing Chinese
shadows against the luminous tumble of greenery and
the dust-haze of the parade ground. And struck by a
sudden long ray as it sank reddish-gold, the little group
shone resplendent and for a moment rose to a kind
of eternity, dresses billowing white as pages, the chairs
dazzling, the drinking-glasses turning to emeralds,
jacinths, rubies.

WHEN I arrive at Zinna's, she is finishing a modest dairy and fruit supper. She rises to her feet – Marie cannot stop her – so shrunken that she barely reaches my navel. I remember that before the War she had been crazy about the film *Naples au baiser de feu*. Bravely I lean down and plant a kiss amid the bristles. Her voice, too, has become masculine, dropping several tones, so that now it rises as if – already – from a tomb. "Do sit down," my aunt tells her, seeing her sway. But Zinna refuses and lurches off. Age with its huge encumbrance has left invisible passages where she advances with a kind of timorous ease, groping her way along quasi-walls, making use even of obstacles, as if she were less at risk of falling than of flying away. And after lengthily negotiating each of the steps leading down from the kitchen, we are in the garden. Through its foliage the evening light splashes onto exuberant flowerbeds in the vegetable patch where once I admired the almost immaterial featheriness of asparagus tops. It is tended by Zinna's son, Paul, who has just joined us. Lithe as a cat, restless as a ferret, always perched on a roof or up a tree – that was the lad I had known, and here he is, solidly planted like an athletic version of his father, who had the same first name as mine and went around with a swagger, back in those days when Zinna wore a plume in her hat and lipstick of the most violent *Baiser* red.

We leave the garden and go a little way along the dead-end lane bounded by those barrack walls with their disconcerting contours. This was once a little Italy – with masons, contractors – where the personal prestige of my grandfather, a mechanic from Piedmont, helped to curb the self-importance of the Ticinesi majority. A little further on, in the big house blighted by its Jules Ferry-cum-pre-Renaissance design, lived Betty Milo. At twelve years of age and each in their own way – like Elizabeth Taylor and Gina Lollobrigida, you might say – she and Paul's sister had perfected the image of the film star while also becoming a focus of attraction and aggressiveness, which was not the case with Annette. They already had sex-appeal. We got excited and spied on them during their innocent dolls' tea-parties; we played tricks on them. They dealt with us condescendingly.

Right now we are quietly chatting about nothing in particular. To hear us, you'd think it was only yesterday we had gone our separate ways – and the day before yesterday, the day before that, and so on across fifty years. What has happened to the time in-between? Once I was here, now I'm here again, and the two instances overlap across an imaginary break. This is surely what we are all thinking, behind our words. The setting, it's true, is identical: the same wide, dusty, cement-grey courtyard surrounding the garden of the country house and opening onto the lane; the same dismal row of storage sheds. Moments of mad joy have subsided behind those wooden doors. Who would dare say: "I remember"? Now that we have finished our small-talk, nobody talks at all; we drift. Then all of a sudden, like a small sleepwalking mummy, Zinna sets off backwards – a bizarre, lurching movement, her legs wobbling. Instinctively I reach out and whisper to alert the others, but Paul shrugs. "Leave her be," he says. "She does it on purpose." And we stand there in silence, not moving, as Zinna retreats ever more swiftly into the brightness of old times.

Monday Evening

COMING back from Zinna's means going past the garage. It was around this hour of the day that we returned from the lake on Sunday, and that I landed here last week. I ask Marie, rather tortuously, if there isn't any more shopping to be done. "Ah yes," she says, "I think we're out of bread." And as if reading my thoughts, she adds: "Take your time. There's no hurry."

On Rue des Bosquets I find a bakery almost right away, and to be on the safe side – most of the shops are beginning to lower their shutters – buy a baguette. The streets are nearly empty and soon I am walking alone, bread in hand, like the child I'd have liked to see when I arrived. I all but skip along, feeling a new lightness, as if I have given my memories back to the town and can simply trot beside her, moved and amazed. I have taken the same route as last time, beyond the castle, and at the risk of coming up against locked gates further on, I return through the park in the lengthening light that probes to the heart of statues and makes them shine. My shadow, as though floating just off the ground, stretches towards the parade ground. Despite the cawing of rooks as hundreds of them gather back into their dormitories, I can hear blackbirds calling back and forth. Their singing seems to crystallize the moment – but so entirely, and with such vehement happiness, it seems to arise from another side of the world, one that's forever bathed in gold and is still to be found at the end of the Cyclists' Path, in the castle windows set ablaze by a different sun.

SKIRTING the school I have wandered across Place Léopold, thinking of the little steam-train I sometimes took on trips to Montcel with my grandmother. I am slowly making my way towards the street I've been avoiding until now. The time has come. No point putting it off: I know I will be leaving tomorrow – and must have known it, without quite grasping the fact, when I passed the garage. Not that I had fixed any departure date. I had simply thought: a few days, maybe a week, I'll see. Time enough to understand.

Well, here I am. Why did I make such an episode of it? Here, too, hardly anything has changed. The number of shops is much as it was, most of them selling the same goods as before – including those famous slippers – and all of them, curiously enough, on the same side of the street. As if some hierarchical code had required a strict partition between the commercial sector and, facing it, the middle-class; on the latter side stood the small building where Fernand lived with his son whom everyone took for my brother. Our old shop is still there, barely recognizable in the new guise of an insurance agency. But it's just as well. I wouldn't really want to see myself slide into transparency this evening amid those rows of phantom bikes, meeting up with other reflections. Besides, if I chose to I could easily wander in my mind's eye through the long series of rooms ending in the workshop, where you had to blow hard into the speaking-tube to hear from the other end an old dog's dreamy sighing. On the way I would rediscover the particular smell of each place; what they all had in common – even in the kitchen, where it was mixed in with coal, tobacco, compote and laundry – was rubber. I would come back through the narrow courtyard and go up to the first floor (the stairs passed over a well where the bogey-man had his lair, so the grown-ups said), follow the dark corridor with the intriguing, tapless stone sink, its plug-hole opening directly onto the dreaded place; glance past the red and black Chinese folding screen that guards the empty darkness of the big room I never entered except in dreams (when it was full of lead soldiers) or – more often – in nightmares that have pursued me across the years. And then the room where my little bed was wedged between that of my parents and the huge, malevolent mirrored wardrobe; the window I sometimes climbed through to venture over the workshop roof towards the big lime tree that on clear summer nights produced a phenomenal new-laid moon, lighting up everything you didn't know. And then downstairs again, across to the far side of the courtyard, past the laundry where Madame Karl had got away with murder, and the shared toilets that Antoine decorated with funny pictures, and turn right to the dead-end where there was a recess we called "the thicket": in part a heap of sand dotted with cat-droppings that my friend Dany and I used to lob over the wall at the kids from the furniture shop, in part a slope where, with the aid of an upturned bike frame that made a passable machine-gun, we liquidated a good few Spanish republican soldiers. Of course, these massacres had no political basis whatsoever, and no explanation besides the fact that in the newspapers their foes were called – so much more dashingly – "rebels", just as in the case of Abyssinia there was wholesale desertion from Mussolini to join the ranks of the Negus.

A few years ago, thanks to Marie who knew one of the residents, I saw the old courtyard again, locked now behind a coded security gate as if to protect the memories of those who used to live there, and wisely deny access to those who still do. And it looked so much the way it always had, there might have been quite a shock in store. But some instinct barred my way, as did the discomfiting presence of the gentleman who – very warily, it seemed to me – let us in, not to mention the company of Marie, who well before my time had scampered about with my father between these sad walls. We stayed no longer than five minutes, and took no more than three steps inside. From a distance I saw – same as ever – the tarred planks of the ever-subsiding workshop, the kitchen door, the well, the stairway where I stood on guard . . .

Enough. The street is already quite blue: what am I waiting for, shouldering my baguette like a wooden rifle? Why should I need things to be actually present? They are within me. And not even like a treasure to be dipped into keenly and cautiously; nor like the dim reservoir of the central pumping-station at Cattenom. Inseparable from all that's being added day by day, still they remain on the surface. It's my baggage. I can leave. Already I find I'm moving on, strolling in the intense evening blue that brings to mind my little crayon and the puppet theatre Francis had, where the set for "The Street" served as backdrop for most of the little plays we made up. But for me, Guignol's squabbles with Gnafron and the Gendarme held less interest than the scenery itself, where nothing would ever happen. I could have gazed at it for hours, as if to go right through it and find that other side which we merely brushed against in town, and which had put me there in the first place.

I have now turned the corner after the slipper shop. I think of the ingenious models and amazing puppets Pascal used to make. I think of Monsieur Jean behind

his window. I keep turning around to see the ever dark-
ening mass of Les Bosquets, and as I pass below other
windows, wonder if there might not be another Mon-
sieur Jean behind each of them. Then suddenly the
street-lamps come on, though the sky is still quite light.
Each lamp-post takes up my shadow in turn; not yet
detached from the one before, it is drawn into the gravi-
tational field of the next, as if being winched in, so that
the shadow is, at one and the same time, chasing me and
running ahead, driving me forward and claiming me
back. After a while it begins to look autonomous, pro-
jected by a whole procession of invisible strangers. Is
this me walking, or the town going about in its own
uninhabited space?

Finally I arrive back, none too proud of myself. Not
only have I given Marie cause for worry, but I have
absent-mindedly chewed both ends of her baguette.

Tuesday Morning

– SO YOU'RE leaving, says Marie.

– Well, the time has come.

And to offset my weak response, I add weakly:

– But I will be back.

– Then I'll let you be on your way, she says. I can't bear seeing people off.

Here I am, alone in the street once more. Checking my pack a last time. Nothing missing. I've given back the key. But a window opens – Marie:

– What about the mirabelles from Gérard?

I go back up. I suspect that after twenty or thirty kilometres the package will be little more than a reeking pulp. But to throw it away would be sacrilege. So I wedge it between my waterproofs and the fuel can, more or less cushioned against jolts and within easy reach. On the road I'll be able to help myself, scattering plum stones as I go.

I will be back.